The Big Green Umbrella

THE BIG GREEN
UMBRELLA

Story by
**ELIZABETH
COATSWORTH**

Illustrated by
**HELEN
SEWELL**

Publishers · **GROSSET & DUNLAP** · New York

THE BIG GREEN UMBRELLA

MR. THOMAS THOMAS had an umbrella. It was a very fine umbrella, made of dark green silk, with an ivory tip and a round ivory handle.

Mr. Thomas's umbrella was a very large umbrella. It was really like a small silk roof. It would keep Mr. Thomas and Mrs. Thomas and young Tom and little Amanda all dry on a rainy day. At least if the rain came down straight, they would be dry.

On rainy days the whole family walked together, under Mr. Thomas's big green umbrella. The umbrella would keep them dry, going to church, or going down the street in the little town of Newcastle, Delaware, under the rows of elm trees, past the little red brick houses with their small-paned windows.

People looking out from upstairs windows would say, "There goes Mr. Thomas's big green umbrella!"

Everyone knew it. There were many big umbrellas in Newcastle, but Mr. Thomas's was the biggest, the greenest, and the silkiest.

He was very proud of it, and so were Mrs. Thomas and young Tom and Amanda.

But one day the umbrella seemed to grow tired of its life in Newcastle. It grew tired of keeping the rain off the Thomases on rainy days and on sunny days standing in the dark corner behind the door. It had heard the talk of the winds from far away. It had listened to the whispering of raindrops which had seen all the world at one time or another. Goodness knows what thoughts the umbrella had been thinking during all the long hours behind the door! But when the moment came, the umbrella acted.

It was a Saturday morning in April. The wind blew fresh, the clouds raced overhead, the sun shone brightly when it shone at all. The birds sat among the budding trees and sang for joy, though sometimes they had to stop their singing when a sudden flurry of wind almost blew their tails inside out. It was a wild day, but a lovely day. The dogs barked, the little boys flew their plunging kites, the horses clattering over the cobbled streets threw up their heads at the blowing bits of paper, and the Thomas family went for a walk. Mr. Thomas took the umbrella along, because in April a shower may come up at any minute.

When people in Newcastle went for a walk, they always went to the river, the Delaware River whose wide waters ran along the back of the gardens of the red brick houses on the strand. There were always things to be seen on the river, a flock of wild ducks bobbing about, or fishermen in their small boats. Or it might be a big clipper ship with its white sails spread, sailing down the river for South America, or the ports of Russia, or far-away China.

On this April morning, such a ship was standing off the shore, its sails taut with wind.

"She's from Philadelphia," Mr. Thomas remarked, "probably bound for the Pagoda Anchorage."

"I wish I were on her," said young Tom.

"So do I," said little Amanda.

"Pooh, you'd be sick!" cried Tom.

"No more than you!" cried Amanda.

"Hush, children," said gentle Mrs. Thomas, "see, it's beginning to rain."

Yes, the clouds had suddenly gathered. A minute ago the sun was shining, and now the rain was falling!

Mr. Thomas put up the big green silk umbrella, and all the Thomases gathered under it like chickens under a bush when the rain begins. Had the umbrella heard what the children said? Who will ever know?

Suddenly an unexpected gust of wind arose, stronger than any of the others. It pushed its way under the green umbrella. Umbrella and wind together struggled to pull the ivory handle out of Mr. Thomas's grasp. They tugged, they jerked, they plunged.

Mrs. Thomas smothered a scream, the children knocked against Mr. Thomas's elbows, the umbrella like a thing gone mad whacked against Mr. Thomas's fine beaver hat and sent it spinning. As Mr. Thomas reached one hand out to catch his hat, the umbrella gave a wicked twist—and it was free! Free with its friend the wind.

Above the meadow the umbrella went, now near the ground, now high in the air, like a big green flower, like a tumbling toadstool. Now it floated like a jellyfish, now it soared upward like a kite, now it turned head-over-heels like a boy at play.

It was over the river now, frightening a flock of ducks which flew up quacking and spattering water.

The rain had stopped already. The sun was out again. In a row the Thomases stood and watched the great green umbrella, which had been their pride, dancing and bowing and pirouetting above the river. Sometimes they couldn't see it and then they would catch a glimpse of it again, dark against the white sails of the clipper ship which it seemed to be approaching. Then they could see it no more.

"If only my hat hadn't blown off!" sighed Mr. Thomas. "I might have held it."

"No one could have held that big umbrella in such a wind," soothed Mrs. Thomas.

"We'll never have another umbrella like that," whimpered Amanda.

"There's not another umbrella like it in the world," said young Tom solemnly.

"The wind's gone down," said Mr. Thomas. "I suppose our umbrella's in the Delaware by now."

"It will float for a while," murmured Mrs. Thomas, "and then I suppose it will sink."

"And scare the fishes," Tom suggested hopefully.

"Perhaps it will keep the sunshine off the fishes as it used to keep the rain off us," said Amanda.

"Anyhow it's at the bottom of the Delaware by now," said Mr. Thomas. "I'm sorry, for it was a fine umbrella. We'll never see it again."

Mr. Thomas was an upright man, a deacon in the church, a kind husband, and an indulgent father. He set the children a splendid example by never making a remark unless he was sure that he was right.

But on this fine blowy April Saturday morning Mr. Thomas was wrong as wrong could be. The umbrella was *not* at the bottom of the Delaware, nor even at the top of it among the waves. And he was mistaken in other ways besides.

Captain John DeWitt of the clipper ship *Commerce* was walking the deck on this fine April morning thinking what a fine ship his was, and what a good crew he had signed on, and how well the first mate was handling the business of sailing the vessel down the river.

Off for China! That was an exciting thought at the beginning of each voyage. To sail halfway round the world and trade with the Chinese, to fill the hold with sweet-smelling tea and buy fine porcelain and embroidered shawls for his wife, surely that was a fine kind of voyage to make.

Suddenly, something caught his eye; it bobbed and winked at the captain.

"That's a funny bird," he thought. But his sharp sailor's eyes told him immediately that it was no bird.

"A kite?" But it hadn't a kite's shape. Dancing, leaping, tumbling, the thing approached nearer.

"An umbrella!" exclaimed the captain and laughed. The umbrella seemed to be on a frolic, so full of high spirits that it couldn't behave the same way for two seconds on end. Now it appeared about to leap into the river, now it changed its course to skim over the masts. At the last moment it did neither, but with a final tumble landed in the rigging and stuck there.

Now a sailor was scrambling up to where the umbrella rested. The thing heaved and moved. It seemed asking the wind not to press it against the ropes but to let it go again to play about in the air. But the wind was a joker, too, turning the umbrella around just as the sailor's brown hand reached for it. Now he had the handle. Now he was working his fingers up to the catch. Now the umbrella had suddenly ceased to be a great green toadstool; it was furled and helpless, only a stick in petticoats.

The sailor brought the closed umbrella to the captain, who examined it.

"A very fine umbrella and not a bit the worse for its cruise," he said. "I'll put it in my cabin and show the Chinese what a good umbrella looks like."

Although the umbrella stood for long weeks behind the cabin door, it was not like standing in the hallway of a house. The air smelled of salt and tarry ropes. The umbrella heard the creaking of cordage and the whistle of wind. It moved up and down, up and down with the motion of the vessel. Although nothing could be seen from the corner of the cabin behind the door, a great deal could be heard and imagined.

Land air has a different smell; first come the sea-birds on the borders of the ocean, and then one hears the land birds singing and twittering. The *Commerce* moved smoothly now on a quiet river. There were cries of men, unlike the sounds of American voices, and smells of gardens and incense and dead fish.

When the *Commerce* came to anchor there were temple bells, too, in the distance, and Chinese voices conferring with Captain DeWitt in the cabin. But still nothing to be seen.

Then one day it rained, slats of rain falling on the cabin roof like a bamboo curtain falling with a sharp sound, and that day the great green umbrella with the ivory handle came out of its hiding and saw China.

If I should tell you all that the umbrella saw, I should have to tell you all about China, for it saw everything. It saw the blue-clothed crowds, with pigtails hanging down their backs, the women with bound feet in little embroidered slippers, the children in bright clothes. It saw the river boats with big eyes painted on each side of the prows, the dark temples opening on streets so narrow that the umbrella touched walls on each side.

Indeed the streets were so very narrow and the green umbrella was so very large that hundreds of Chinese had to pass under it as it moved along, and they all gave it a glance of interest and admiration.

The merchant who was in charge of loading the *Commerce* looked at the umbrella with interest and admiration too.

"A very fine umbrella," he said in Chinese.

"A very fine umbrella," the interpreter repeated in English.

"It is yours," declared Captain DeWitt, for the captain and the merchant were always giving each other presents.

So that afternoon the umbrella started off with a slim yellow hand on its ivory handle, and a grave Chinese face like an old idol's in its green shade.

When the merchant reached his home, he went directly into the part of his house where the women of the family lived, to show them the new umbrella, for the women liked to see things which came from across the

sea. They were used to smaller parasols made of glazed paper. They laughed and stared at the great big green umbrella as large as a little, little house.

Peach Blossom, the merchant's youngest daughter, was more interested than anyone else. "It is so curious," she exclaimed. "I have never seen such a thing."

The merchant smiled at her. "It is yours," he said, "but you must have one of the servants hold it for you when it rains. It is too large for your little hands."

So the umbrella became Peach Blossom's. It went out into the garden in the courtyard to keep her dry when it rained. A big peasant woman held it, while Peach Blossom tripped along on her tiny feet, with food for the goldfish in the rain-speckled pond under the moon-shaped bridge. More rarely it took her to a temple or to visit at some other house where her relatives lived.

Then all the children crowded under the umbrella and laughed because they had seen nothing like it before.

A month went by and one afternoon the merchant noticed that Peach Blossom was looking more thoughtful than usual.

"What are you thinking about, Peach Blossom?" he asked.

"I had a dream last night, my father," Peach Blossom replied, bowing.

"Tell me," he said.

Again Peach Blossom bowed. "I dreamed," she went on, "I was walking out in the rain, holding the foreign umbrella in my hand. And I heard it sigh and I looked up. It seemed then that it was a huge bird which was struggling to get away. But I was not afraid.

"'Why do you sigh?' I asked, and it replied, 'I am weary for my own place and my own people.'

"Then I looked again and it seemed to be only the

foreign umbrella. But this morning when Green Bamboo held it over me during a shower, it tugged and struggled so that she could hardly hold it."

The merchant nodded slowly. "It is homesick," he said. "Things can no doubt be homesick too. I will take it back to the Captain and explain. If it stayed here it would not be lucky. Fortunately the *Commerce* has not yet sailed."

So that was how it came about that the big green umbrella found itself once more behind the door in the captain's cabin. Once more it smelled and heard and felt the life of a ship, leaving the port for the open sea. Once more it shared in the life of a long voyage, heard the talk and felt the rise and fall of the vessel beneath it. Once more it came through storms and calms to the quiet of a great river, but this time the odors that blew from the land and the far-off sounds of the shores were as familiar as sun and rain to the umbrella.

Then once more the ship came up into the wind and the anchor chains rattled and the captain's gig was lowered and the captain and the umbrella were rowed ashore across the bright ripples of the river.

At the little Newcastle customs house the officer bowed politely to Captain DeWitt. "I trust that you had a good voyage to China, sir. Are you putting goods ashore at Newcastle this trip?"

Captain DeWitt laughed. "Only this stowaway which

signed on from here without papers," and he held out the big green umbrella.

"By thunder, sir, that's Mr. Thomas's umbrella which blew away over a year ago. It was the biggest umbrella in town. He never expected to lay eyes on that again, I do assure you."

So the captain explained how the umbrella had chosen to come aboard and the customs officer laughed and nodded, and called a boy.

"Here, Jim, take this to Mr. Thomas's house with my compliments, and tell him that it went on a voyage to China along with Captain DeWitt on the *Commerce*. In China, it was given to a little Chinese girl who had a dream and sent it back because she thought the umbrella was homesick. Amanda will like to hear that."

"Tell Amanda that the little girl's name was Peach Blossom and that she was eight years old," Captain DeWitt joined in.

"That's about Amanda's age," said the customs

officer, "or thereabouts. Children keep changing their ages so fast, I can't keep track of them."

The boy, Jim, started up the street under the elms, whistling and swinging the big green umbrella by its ivory handle. It was so tall he had to keep his hand above his shoulder so the ivory tip wouldn't hit the paving stones.

"What have you got there, Jim?" one of his friends asked him. "Look out or it will run away with you."

"That's Mr. Thomas's green umbrella and it's been on a cruise to China," Jim explained.

"Whew!" said the boy falling in beside Jim, "what do you know about that?"

Just then a lady who was passing stopped, looking sharply at the umbrella. "Isn't that Mr. Thomas's big green umbrella?" she demanded. "What are you doing with it, boy?"

When she heard the story, she nodded her head a couple of times.

"I'll go along to see that you don't break it," she declared. "I do want to see Mrs. Thomas's face when she comes to the door. I've seen that umbrella too many times from my window to be mistaken about it."

So the umbrella went on its triumphant way, and more and more people joined the procession. There were children and dogs of course, and grown-up people too, just to see what the Thomases would say when they saw their big green umbrella returned from faraway China.

Jim knocked on the big shiny knocker on the white door, and the maid came, and was soon followed by

Mr. and Mrs. Thomas and young Tom and little Amanda, pouring out onto the steps to see the big green umbrella. Mr. Thomas opened it, and there it was, as big and sheltering as ever and not a tear or wear in all its dark green surface.

Mrs. Thomas kept repeating, "Well, I never in all my born days!"

Young Tom grinned and went out into the street to see the *Commerce* standing offshore, with her sails set for Philadelphia.

But Amanda went over when no one was looking and kissed the handle of the runaway umbrella to welcome it home again.

It was she who found fastened below the ivory handle a colored cord from which hung an embroidered peach with a tassel at its end, filled with sandalwood, as a remembrance.

But Peach Blossom must have been right: the umbrella apparently wanted to be home where it belonged. For never again did it attempt to leave Newcastle, where it lived in great splendor as the umbrella which had been to China; yes, and had come back again.